Written by Adonis Cole
Copyright © Adonis Cole 2021

All rights reserved. No part of this publication may be reproduced, distributed, or transmitted in any form by any means, including photocopying, recording, or other electronic or mechanical methods, without the prior written permission of the publisher, except in the case of brief quotations embodied in critical reviews and certain other noncommercial uses permitted by copyright law

Illustrated by Olivia Maria Chevallier
Artworks © Olivia Maria Chevallier 2021

Illustrator's contact details:
W: www.OliviaChevallier.art

ISBN: 9798470797520
Independently published

First Edition

Dedicated to my daughter Sophia,
remembering reading her bedtime stories

Basil and Olive

Written by A. Cole

Illustrated by Olivia Chevallier

There's this cute grey mouse called Basil,

    Who lives in the tiniest hole,

He likes to hang out with Olive,

    A kind and cute little mole.

Each morning when Basil wakes up,

    He stretches his arms to the sky,

The yawns and noises from this tiny mouse,

    Show his mouth as wide as a pie!

2

He sits and ponders with a smile,

    Of the joy he will have this day,

But 'til he's eaten some cheese and scraps,

    There's nothing much he'll say...

At times he seems slightly grumpy,

    If he's not eaten his morning delights,

This doesn't look good for the big people though,

    Because if hungry, he could give them a fright.

4

But it's rare that he appears scary,

    As he always finds food to eat,

Just by stepping out of his little house,

    There is plenty down by his feet.

His best friend Olive, however,

    Has everything under control,

She safely stores all of her food,

    Whilst she's alert and on patrol.

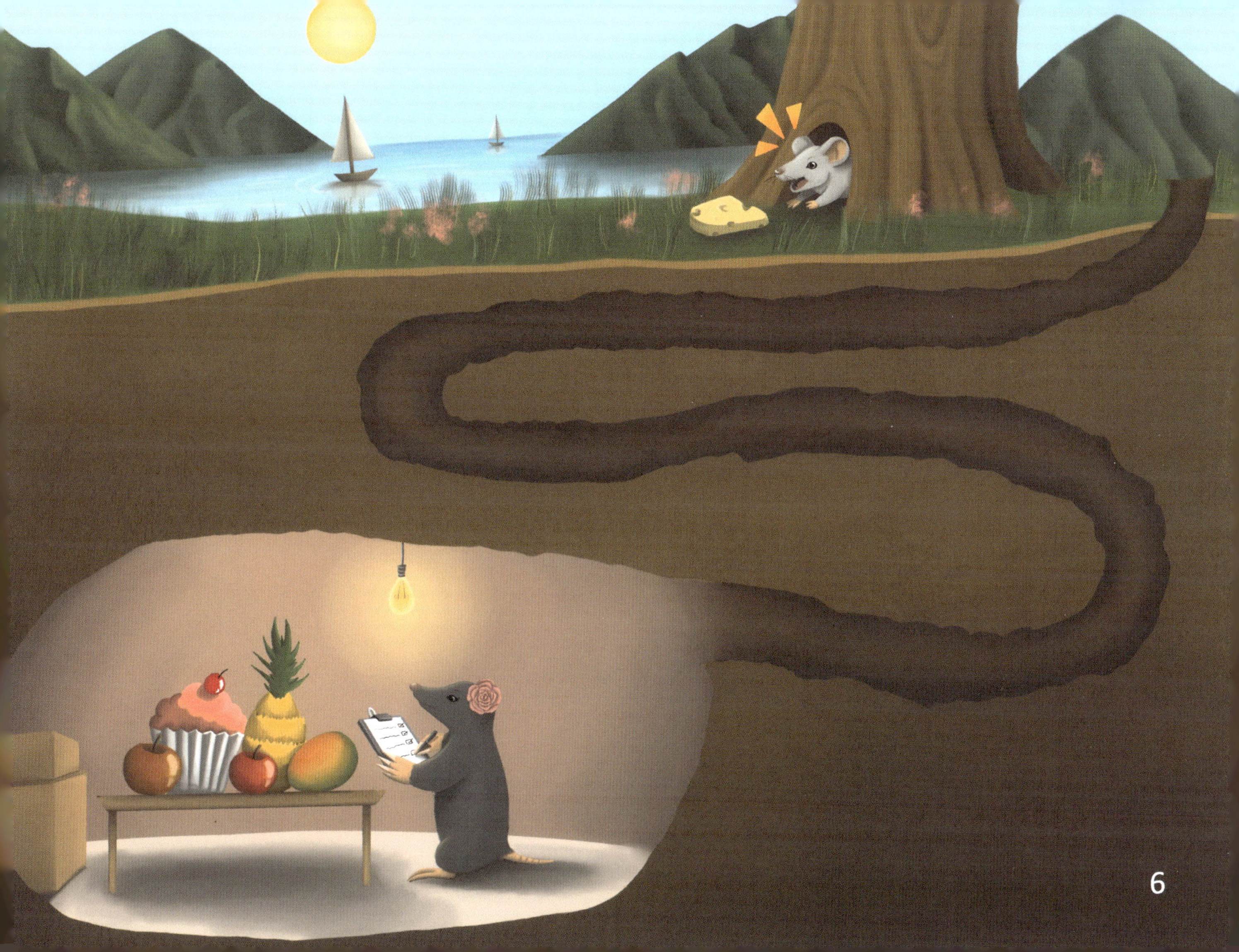

Olive, is a very wise mole,

    Since her house is way underground,

She hides her food deep in the tunnels,

    When nobody's lurking around.

Together, these two are best friends,

    And love to meet up each day,

They start to plan the adventures they'll have,

    And the games they hope to play.

8

Jumping and hiding in the leaves,

    When nobody else is around,

As this is their favourite hiding place,

    And their own special playground.

They race and chase and climb up the trees,

    And then sprint their way down holes,

Visiting some of the neighbouring tunnels,

    And greeting the numerous moles.

10

They often meet with many friends,
    Like rabbits, squirrels and toads,
One thing, however, they never forget,
    Is to mind those dangerous roads.

When the day is almost ending,
    And it's time to go their own way,
They smile and shout to each other...
    "See you tomorrow for another play?"

12

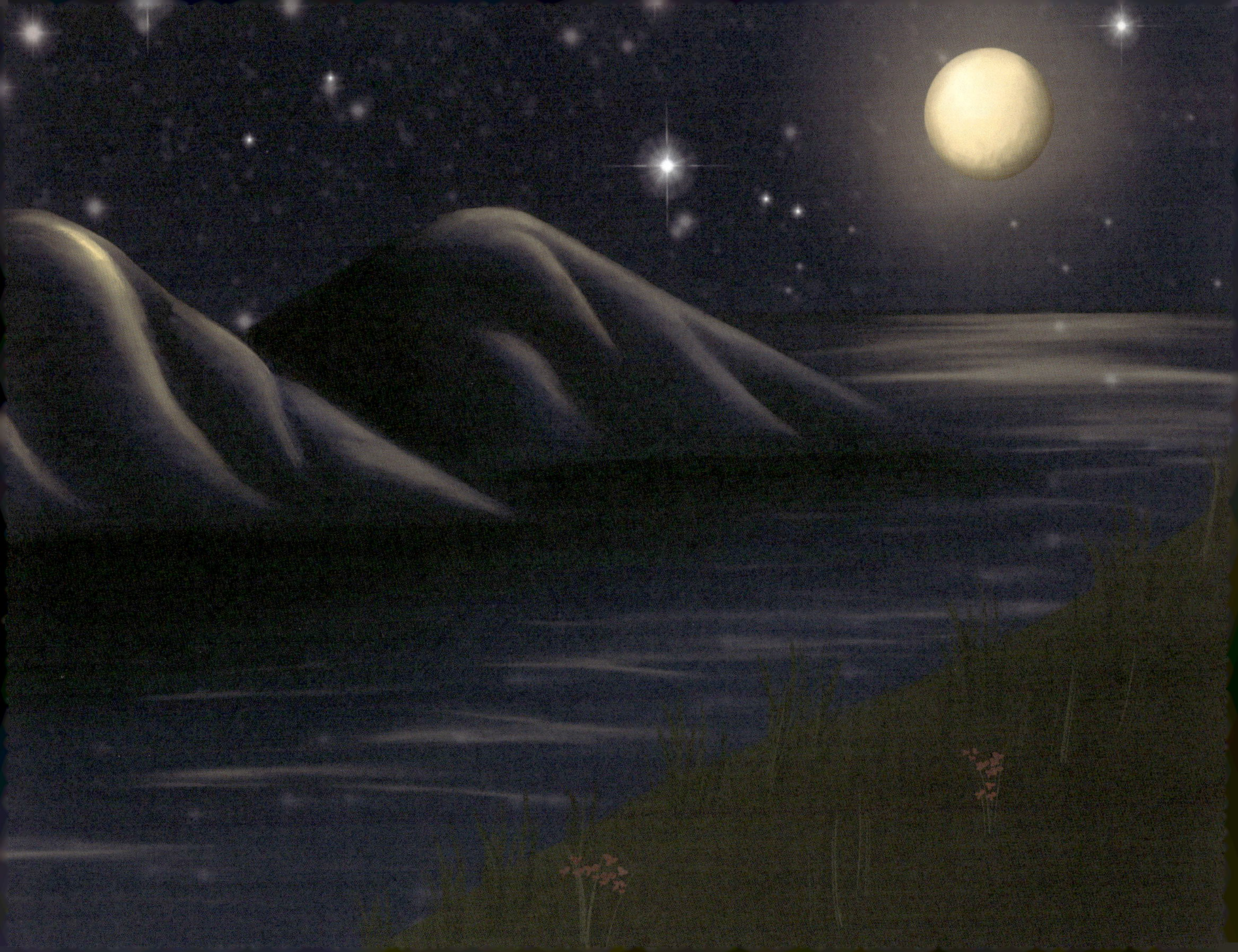

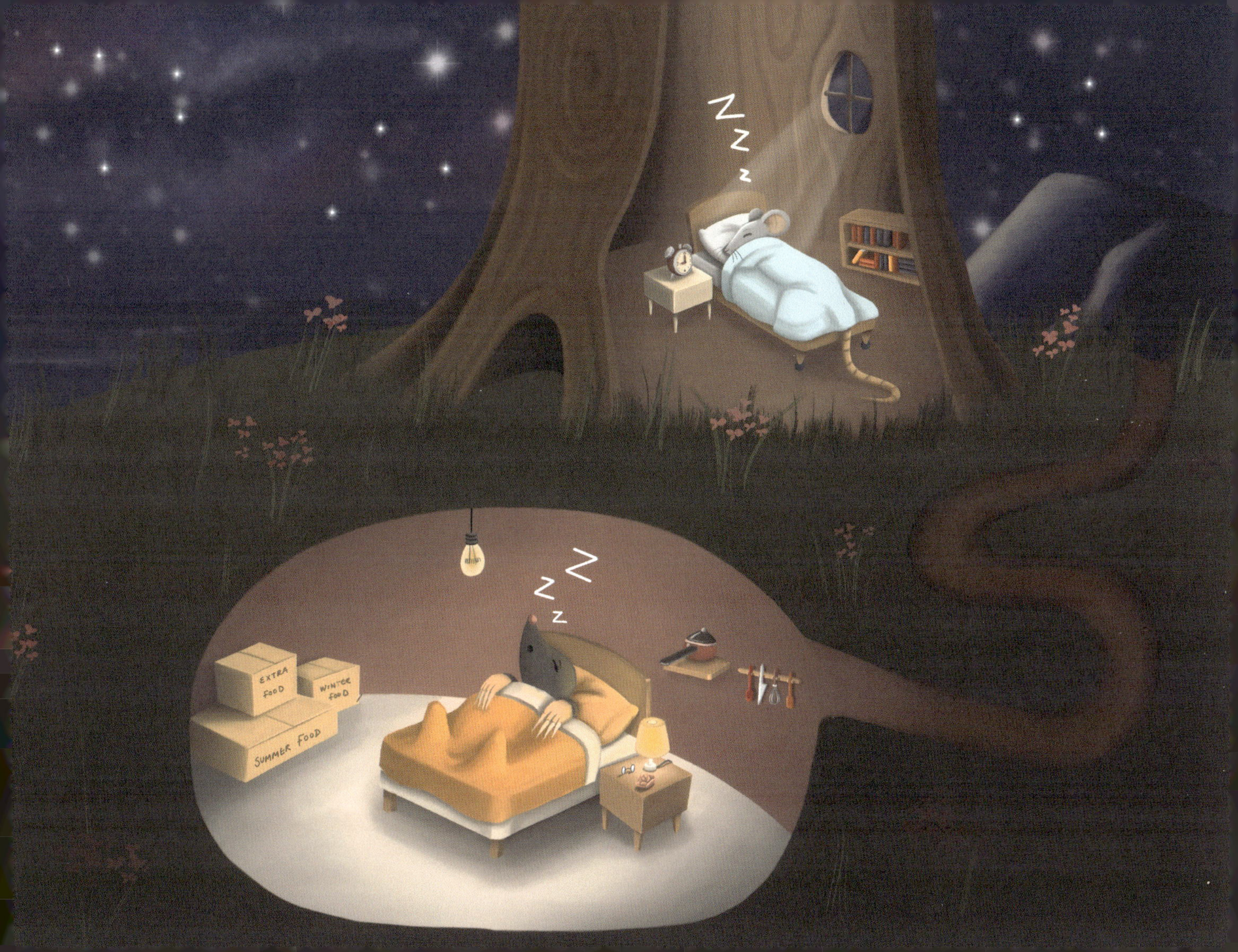
EXTRA FOOD
WINTER FOOD
SUMMER FOOD

Goodnight...

16

To Anna

Enjoy

A Dorif

Printed in Great Britain
by Amazon

67774144R00015